**Dear Parents,**

Welcome to the Scholastic Reader series. We have taken over 80 years of experience with teachers, parents, and children and put it into a program that is designed to match your child's interests and skills.

**Level 1**—Short sentences and stories made up of words kids can sound out using their phonics skills and words that are important to remember.

**Level 2**—Longer sentences and stories with words kids need to know and new "big" words that they will want to know.

**Level 3**—From sentences to paragraphs to longer stories, these books have large "chunks" of texts and are made up of a rich vocabulary.

**Level 4**—First chapter books with more words and fewer pictures.

It is important that children learn to read well enough to succeed in school and beyond. Here are ideas for reading this book with your child:

- Look at the book together. Encourage your child to read the title and make a prediction about the story.
- Read the book together. Encourage your child to sound out words when appropriate. When your child struggles, you can help by providing the word.
- Encourage your child to retell the story. This is a great way to check for comprehension.
- Have your child take the fluency test on the last page to check progress.

Scholastic Readers are designed to support your child's efforts to learn how to read at every age and every stage. Enjoy helping your child learn to read and love to read.

—**Francie Alexander**
Chief Education Officer
Scholastic Education

*For David*
*—Aunt Gracie*

No part of this publication may be reproduced, or stored in a retrieval system, or transmitted in any form or by any means, electronic, mechanical, photocopying, recording, or otherwise, without written permission of the publisher. For information regarding permission, write to Scholastic Inc., Attention: Permissions Department, 557 Broadway, New York, NY 10012.

ISBN 0-439-40570-X

Text copyright © 2003 by Grace Maccarone.
Illustrations copyright © 2003 by Norman Bridwell.
All rights reserved. Published by Scholastic Inc.
SCHOLASTIC, CARTWHEEL BOOKS, and associated logos
are trademarks and/or registered trademarks of Scholastic Inc.

Library of Congress Cataloging-in-Publication Data is available.

10  9  8  7  6                                                    06  07
Printed in the U.S.A.  23 • First printing, May 2003

# MAGIC MATT ™
### and the Skunk in the Tub

by **Grace Maccarone**

Illustrated by **Norman Bridwell**

## Scholastic Reader — Level 1

SCHOLASTIC INC.

New York   Toronto   London   Auckland   Sydney
Mexico City   New Delhi   Hong Kong   Buenos Aires

Hello! I am Magic Matt.
I can do magic.
I can make a garden.
Zap!

See me water the garden.
Zap!

Oh, no!
I am full of mud.
I need a bath.

I won't use magic for this.
I will just get into the tub.

I want a duck
in the tub.

See me make a duck.
Zap!

No! That is a truck.
I want a duck.
Zap!

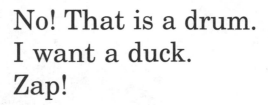

No! That is a drum.
I want a duck.
Zap!

And that is a bug.
Zap!

Oh, no! Oh, no! Oh, no!
That is a skunk!

# The skunk makes a stink!

Go away!
Zap!

The skunk is gone,
but he left his stink.
Now I stink, too!

I know what to do.

See me make a garden
in the tub.
Zap!

I did it!
And I smell so sweet.

I am clean at last!
Next time, I will take a shower.

# Magic Matt's Magic Words

Up, mud, tub, fun, duck, truck, drum, bug, and skunk all have the "u" sound.

Read these other words that have the "u" sound.

run

sun

bun

bud

bus

but

cup

pup

us

# Fluency Fun

The words in each list below end in the same sounds.
Read the words in a list.
Read them again.
Read them faster.
Try to read all 12 words in one minute.

| | | |
|---|---|---|
| **bun** | **bug** | **duck** |
| **fun** | **dug** | **luck** |
| **run** | **hug** | **truck** |
| **sun** | **rug** | **stuck** |

Look for these words in the story.

| | | |
|---|---|---|
| **to** | **for** | **me** |
| | **see** | **and** |

---

**Note to Parents:**

According to *A Dictionary of Reading and Related Terms*, fluency is "the ability to read smoothly, easily, and readily with freedom from word-recognition problems." Fluency is necessary for good comprehension and enjoyable reading. The activities on this page include a speed drill and a sight-recognition drill. Speed drills build fluency because they help students rapidly recognize common syllables and spelling patterns in words, and they're fun! Sight-recognition drills help students smoothly and accurately recognize words. Practice these activities with your child to help him or her become a fluent reader.

—**Wiley Blevins**,
Reading Specialist